Adventures of Sindbad the Sailor

Simplified by D K Swan
Illustrated by Andrew Brown

Longman

Longman Group UK Limited,
Longman House, Burnt Mill, Harlow,
Essex CM20 2JE, England
and Associated Companies throughout the world.

First published 1987
Seventh impression 1992

ISBN 0-582-54148-4

Set in 12/14 point Linotron 202 Versailles
Printed in Hong Kong
SC/07

Acknowledgements

The cover background is a wallpaper design called NUAGE, courtesy of Osborne and Little plc.

Stage 1: 500 word vocabulary

Please look under *New words* at the back of this book for explanations of words outside this stage.

Contents

Introduction

The Sindbad stories come from the *Arabian Nights* (or the *Thousand and One Nights* – or in Arabic *Alf Leila wa Leila*).

The first book of the *Arabian Nights* in Arabic was written more than a thousand years ago (about the year 940, or AH 330). We think that the Sindbad stories were added after that. But even a thousand years ago the Arabic-speaking people loved to hear stories about voyages to far-away places.

Arab sailors did go to far-away lands. Even 1,200 years ago there were very many Arab merchants in Canton and other cities in China. We know about them from Chinese writing as well as from Arabic books. We know a lot about the journeys and voyages of real men like Suleiman al-Tajir (Suleiman the Merchant). A book about him was written in 851. He told people in Arab lands a lot about China and India and South-East Asia. People in Europe learned about them only after the journeys of Marco Polo between 1271 and 1295.

The Arabs of a thousand years ago knew a lot about the world – much more than the people of Europe knew at that time. The people of Europe had lost the books and maps of Ptolemy (made about 1,800 years ago), but the Arabs had not. They read Ptolemy's work, and they added to the things that he knew.

Arab sailors knew about the monsoons, the winds that blow from the south-west between April and October, and from the north-east between October and April. So they began their voyages to the east in April or May, and they began to sail home from the east in October or November.

The Sindbad stories put the story-tellers' giants and enormous birds and magic into the stories of real voyages and places. People believed – some people still believe – stories about valleys of diamonds, about places where the elephants go to die, about great kings in unknown lands.

Do we believe in the great King Mihraj, who was Sindbad's friend on his first voyage? There were great kings called Maharaja in India a thousand years ago. Mihraj and Maharaja look very nearly the same in some Arabic writing.

Was there a great King of Serendip? Yes. We know that Serendip was the old name for Sri Lanka, and we know that Arab and other merchants did go to that island. Books about the real journeys of Arabs like Suleiman al-Tajir and Ibn Batuta of Fez tell us that Serendip was well known. Its great city of Anuradhapura was the richest in that part of Asia.

On Sindbad's seventh voyage, he was sold by pirates to a merchant. Things like that did happen. People were really afraid of the pirates in the seas of South-East Asia.

The Sindbad stories, then, are like some other great stories of journeys and voyages, part real and part unreal. Today we know a lot about the real countries of the Earth, so what takes the place of the valley of diamonds, the roc's egg, and the land of the monkey-men? Can it be *Star Wars, Doctor Who,* and *The Planet of the Apes?*

The First Voyage

Sindbad the Sailor lived in Baghdad in the time of the great Khalif, Harun al-Rashid.

Sindbad was a very rich man. He had a beautiful house in the best part of the city. And when the sun was hot in the afternoon, he and his friends sat under the trees in the garden.

"I am rich," he told his friends, "but I haven't always been rich. I have been very poor, often unhappy, and very often afraid. I was very much afraid on my first voyage. I'll tell you about it."

I was a young man at the time. Like many young men, I lived foolishly, and soon I hadn't much money.

"I must do something to get more money," I told myself.

So I sold my house and all my things for three thousand dirhams. With that money, I bought a lot of the best cloth and other goods. I took them to Basra. There was an Arab ship in the river there, and I spoke to its captain.

"We are going to sail next week," he told me. "There will be six merchants with their goods on the ship, and we shall sail to the countries and islands of the far east. There the merchants will sell their goods. They will buy the jewels and other rich things of the east, and they will sell them in their own countries when we come back here."

"Can you take one more merchant?" I asked. And I added, "I have only a few boxes of goods. And I'll give you most of the money I get."

"Yes, I can take you," the captain said.

And so, the next week, we sailed down the great river, the Shatt al-Arab, and through the Gulf, and then towards the east.

We sailed for very many days and nights, and we stopped at cities and islands to sell and buy goods.

One day we came to a very beautiful island.

"I don't know this island at all," the captain said. "But it looks good, and it may have good water."

He brought the ship very near to the land, and a lot of us went on to the island to look for water and to walk about. The seamen took big water pots from the ship with them. I wanted to see the other side of the island, and I began to walk away from the ship. Some of the other merchants found wood, and they made a fire on the land, not far from the ship.

Then two things happened at the same time. The island moved! And the captain shouted: "Run! Run to the ship! It isn't an island at all. It's a great

The island moves!

fish. It has been sleeping on top of the water for years, and so plants have grown on it. But your fire has woken it. Run!"

We ran. But I had a long way to run. Before I could get to the ship, the island-fish went down – down – far down into the sea.

At the same time, a great wind came. It took the ship far away. When at last I got to the top of the water, I couldn't even see the ship.

"Am I going to die here, alone in the great sea?" I thought.

But – Allah is good! – I saw a big water pot near me, and I put my arms round it.

The water pot saved me, but it was hard to stay with it: the sea threw us about so much.

Night came. The wind drove me, with the water pot, all that night, and all the next day and the next night. In the morning, I looked round me.

"This is my last day," I thought. "I'm cold and ill, and only just alive. My fingers are dead, and my arms will soon be dead too. I'll lose the water pot and go down for ever into the sea."

And then I saw it – land!

The wind took me, with the water pot, to the land, and the sea threw me under a tree there. After that, I don't remember things well. I think I couldn't move for two days.

"I must find food and water," I told myself.

"I'll die if I don't."

So I tried to stand up. . . . I couldn't. I looked at my feet, and I saw the places where fish had bitten them.

"They'll be better in time," I thought. "But I must wash them in clean water. I *must* find water."

I moved myself along the ground with my arms, and at last I found a place where one fruit tree grew by a little river. I stayed there for a few days. I ate the fruit from the tree and I drank the water of the little river. My feet grew better, and I myself grew stronger.

It was time to move. I took some fruit with me, but I couldn't take any water.

"There will be other rivers," I thought.

But there was no other drinking water, and there were no other fruit trees. I walked along beside the sea, and I saw no houses, no people – nothing. After walking for three days, I began to be afraid.

"Am I alone," I asked myself, "in a land without people? Is it a place with no beasts, no birds, no living thing? – But what's that?"

It was far away, but it was a horse!

I walked towards the horse, and I saw that it was a very beautiful one.

"A horse like this," I thought, "is a king's or a very rich man's horse."

Just then a man came running from a cave.

He had a sword in his hand, and as he ran he called, "Any man who touches the king's horse dies!"

"Don't kill me," I said. "I was just looking at this beautiful horse. Is it yours?"

"Who are you?" he asked. "And why are you here?"

"I am here," I said, "because Allah was good and sent me a water pot to save me from the sea." And I told him the story.

He took my hand and led me to the cave. There he made me sit down, and he gave me food and water.

"Allah has really been good to you," he said. "For one week every year, I and some other servants of the king bring his best horses here to this island. The air is good for them, but the island has no food or water for men. It is very far from the places where people live, and you would never find your way there without help. We go tomorrow, and you can come with us."

After a time, the other servants came, each with a horse. They heard my story and they were kind to me.

The next day I went with them, riding one of the king's beautiful horses. On the way they told me about their king.

"King Mihraj," they said, "is the greatest king in the land. He is loved by all his people, and he is kind and just to everyone. Merchants from every country come to our great city, which stands beside the sea."

When we got to the city, the servants told King Mihraj about me. The king sent for me and heard my story.

"You have been very fortunate," he said to me. "Allah is good!" And he told his servants to help me in every way.

King Mihraj liked me. He sent for me again and again, and he was very kind to me. I can speak to people from many countries, so he asked me to look after all the merchants and seamen who came to his city. After that, I saw him every day to tell him about the goods that they brought and took away.

I asked the captain of every ship about his voyage and about Baghdad.

One day, a big ship came in from the east. The merchants brought their goods out of it and began selling and buying in the city.

I spoke to the ship's captain. "Are there any more goods in the ship?" I asked.

"These merchants have no more goods in the ship," he said. "But there are a few boxes. A young merchant began the voyage with us, and the goods in the boxes were his. But he is dead. We saw the sea take him. I am going to sell his goods here for gold and take the gold back to his people in the great city of Baghdad."

Then I saw that I knew the captain's face.

"What was his name?" I asked. "What was the merchant's name?"

"His name was Sindbad."

I nearly fell to the ground. I gave a great cry.

"I am Sindbad," I said. "The goods are mine, and I must thank you for saving them for me."

"Oh!" he cried. "Who can we believe? You have the look of a good man, but you say that you are Sindbad. You say it because you want his goods. Sindbad is dead. I saw the sea take him, and the seamen and merchants on my ship saw him die too."

"Captain," I said, "hear my story, and then you will believe me." And I told him my story from the time that I spoke to him at Basra. I told him the words that we had spoken, and I made him remember many things that he and I had said and done.

At last he believed me, and he and the merchants from the ship were very glad.

"We didn't believe that you could be alive," they said. "But Allah is good, and we are very happy that you have been saved."

Then the captain gave me all my goods. I made from them a rich present for King Mihraj, and the seamen carried it to him and put it down at his feet.

"What is this?" the king said to me. "You came here with nothing, and now, so soon, you can give me this very rich present. How has this happened?"

I told him about the ship which had come with my own goods. He gave thanks to Allah for me, and he gave me a present that was far better than my present to him.

When the ship was ready to sail, I went to see King Mihraj.

"I am sad," I told him, "to go from your beautiful country and from its great and good king – from you who have been so kind to me. But I must see again my own dear city of Baghdad."

"Yes, Sindbad," he said. "You must go home. You have been a good friend, and you have helped me greatly. Go with my thanks."

King Mihraj told his servants to take rich presents to the ship for me: gold and jewels, beautiful cloths, and other things without price.

After a very long voyage, the ship came to Basra, and I soon made the journey to Baghdad. My friends were glad to see me, and I bought a beautiful house and lived there, rich and happy, for some years.

Tomorrow, if Allah wills, I shall tell you about my second voyage.

The Second Voyage

I thought that I had come home to Baghdad to live there for ever. I was very happy in my beautiful house. I had friends and servants and everything that riches bring.

But the wish to see more countries and cities and to buy and sell in far-away places grew stronger and stronger. At last I filled very many boxes with all the best goods that one can find in Baghdad, and I sailed, with other merchants, on a beautiful, new ship.

We had a good voyage, sailing from place to place, and from island to island, always going towards the south and east.

After a long time, we came to a beautiful island. It was full of green trees, and fruit, and flowers, and rivers of good, clean water. But there were no people to be seen – no people at all.

Some of the seamen went to get clean water, and some merchants wanted to walk about on land. I went with them on to the island.

The flowers were really beautiful. I went through the trees to look at some very big flowers of great beauty, and I think that the smell of those flowers made me fall asleep.

When I woke up, I was alone. There were no seamen and no other people to be seen.

"What a fool I am!" I cried. "Why did I come away from my beautiful home in Baghdad? Here I am again, alone in a land without people!"

But then I thought, "I am in the hands of Allah. It is foolish to cry out and do nothing."

By hard work I got to the top of a tree, and I looked around me.

Far out over the sea, I saw our ship sailing away from the island. On the island itself I saw nothing but trees – trees – trees. I looked and looked.

There was one thing – a big thing – far away, that was not green. It was white, and like a great round dome on the top of a house.

I walked towards it – many hours' walk. At last I came to it in the evening. It was like an enormous egg.

"If it is a dome," I thought, "where is the house? Where is the door?"

As I was looking at it, something shut out the light of the sun.

"This is like night," I thought. And I looked up.

What I saw was an enormous bird.

Then I remembered the stories that seamen told about a great bird called a roc, or *rukh*. "Rocs are so big," the seamen said, "that they give elephants to their young to eat."

"So this," I thought, "is a roc's egg, and the roc has come to sit on it."

The great bird did sit on the egg, and it went to sleep there.

"Where has it come from?" I asked myself. "And where will it go? It may go to a place where there are men, and that would be better than this place where there are no people."

I took the turban from my head and put it round my body and round the roc's leg, which was like a tree. And then I waited.

When morning came, the roc took me up, up into the sky. It did not know that I was there, and it took me a long, long way over seas and islands and hills and valleys. At last it came down in a great valley with hills like great walls on each side.

The roc came down on an enormous snake. I was really afraid then, and I took my turban off the roc's leg, and ran to hide by a great stone. The roc took the snake up into the air. And then I looked round me.

There were other enormous snakes in the valley. Some of them were as long as a ship. But they were all going into great holes in the ground.

"They sleep in these holes by day," I thought, "and come out to get their food by night. So in the daytime I mustn't be afraid to look for a place to get out of the valley."

But there was no place where I could get up

the sides of that valley. I walked along it, and I saw that the valley floor was made of nothing but diamonds. They were very good diamonds, very big and beautiful. But I didn't want them; I wanted to get out of the valley.

Night came, and I saw the great snakes beginning to come out of their holes. Fortunately I was near a small cave. I ran to it and went inside. There was a big stone there, and I moved it into the mouth of the cave.

That stone saved me. All night I heard the noise of the snakes – *Sssssss*! – round the cave, but they couldn't get to me.

In the morning, I came out of the cave.

"I *must* find a way out of the valley," I thought. And I began to look again.

There was a great thump on the ground near me, and I saw a very big bit of meat on the diamonds. It was red where knives had cut it. Then I remembered the stories that I had heard about the Valley of Diamonds.

Merchants can't go down into the valley to get the diamonds. So they cut up beasts and throw them down. The meat falls on the diamonds. The sun makes the meat sticky, and some diamonds – but not the biggest ones – stick to it. They have some very big birds in that country. The great birds come, and they take the big bits of meat and fly up with them to their young ones on the hills. The merchants make a big noise, and the birds fly away. Then the merchants take the diamonds that have stuck to the meat.

"A bird brought me here," I said to myself, "so a bird can take me away."

I had a bag that I carried food in, and I filled the bag with the biggest and best diamonds. Then I took off my turban again, and I put it round my body and round the biggest bit of meat. I waited there on my back, with the meat on top of me.

After a time, one of the great birds flew down. It took the bit of meat and flew up out of the valley with it – and with me.

At the top of a hill by the side of the valley, the bird's young were waiting. But the merchants were waiting too. They made a great noise, and the bird flew away. Then the merchants came to get the diamonds. I stood up – all red from the meat, and ill after my two journeys through the air.

The merchants were afraid when they saw me, but I told them not to be afraid.

"I am a man," I said, "like you. But the bird that brought your meat brought me up from the Valley of Diamonds. There are no diamonds on your meat, but I have brought diamonds with me. Each one is better than all the diamonds that your meat could bring, and I will gladly give you some of them."

Sindbad stands up – all red from the meat

After that, they came to me and spoke kindly to me.

"You are fortunate," they said. "No other man has ever come back from that valley."

"I give thanks to Allah," I said.

The merchants helped me to sell some of my diamonds and to find a ship to take me to my own country.

At last I came home to Baghdad, a very rich man, with the biggest of my diamonds and other goods.

"Now I'll stay at home here," I told myself, "in my beautiful house, with all my riches. I'll be happy with my friends, and I'll never go to sea again."

But I *did* go to sea again. Tomorrow, if Allah wills, I'll tell you about my third voyage.

The Third Voyage

How foolish a man can be! It was not long before I had again the wish to see other countries and to buy and sell goods in them.

I soon sailed from Basra with other merchants in a very good ship. We went from country to country and from island to island, and we did well everywhere. We were soon rich and very pleased with our voyage.

Then one day a strong wind began to take us where we did not want to go. For four days we were driven by the great wind, and at last we found ourselves beside an island.

The captain spoke to us. We could see by his face that he was really afraid.

"We can't sail away into this wind," he said. "But I know about this island. Its people are small and they are like monkeys. They come on to ships in thousands – thousands and thousands of them. If a man tries to stop them, very many of them fight and kill him. Please, please don't fight them."

As he stopped speaking, the monkey-men came. They came in their thousands, and we couldn't do anything to stop them. They were soon all over the ship. They made all the sailors and merchants go on to the island, and then they sailed our ship away to another part of the island.

"There are more monkey-men on the island," we thought. "What can we do? Where can we go?"

From the top of a tree, one of the sailors saw a big stone house. "Shall we go there to hide from the monkey-men?" he said.

The house had one very big hall, and we all went into it through the great door. We were waiting there when we heard the feet of a giant coming towards us.

He came into the hall and shut the door so we couldn't get out. He was enormous – like a man but as big as a great tree, with eyes like fire, and teeth like great white stones in a mouth like a cave. He took wood from a great box of firewood in the hall and made a big fire. Then he looked at us.

He took me up in his hands, but he found that I was not a fat man. Fortunately, under my rich clothes, I was really not fatter than his finger. So he threw me down and took up another man. In that way he took up one man after another, and at last he found the fattest.

He cooked that man over his fire! Then he ate him! Then he sat down near the fire and went to sleep.

The next day, he went out of the hall, but he

The giant finds the fattest man

shut the great door, and we couldn't get out.

In the evening, the giant came back. Again he took up one man after another, and at last he found a strong man – the ship's captain. And he cooked him! And ate him! And went to sleep.

In the morning, the giant went out and shut the door again.

"We must do something," I said, "or he will eat all of us, one at a time. He is too big for us to kill when he is awake." And I told them what I thought we must do.

That evening the giant came into the hall. He took a man, cooked and ate him, and went to sleep.

Then we began to work quickly.

Two men put long bits of iron into the fire and made them red-hot. Two other men worked with wood from the fire to burn a way through the door. The others used wood from the giant's firewood box to make parts of boats.

When everything was ready, I called out, "Now!"

We drove the red-hot iron into the giant's eyes, and then we all ran, with the boat parts, out of the hall and down to the sea. The giant's cries rang in our ears!

We made our boats, and we had just moved them out to sea when the giant was led down to the waterside by two of his friends.

When they saw us, they took up great stones

and threw them at us. Each stone was as big as a house. Some of them fell into the sea, but some hit our boats and killed the men in them.

One boat – the boat that I was in – was not hit. We worked hard to take it out to sea, but then a strong wind came and drove us along, day after day, through angry seas, before we were thrown up on an island.

Only three of us were alive by that time. We had had no food or water for a long time, but we were alive. We found fruit trees and a small river, and we ate and drank and gave thanks. Then, because our journey in the boat had been so bad, we fell asleep on the ground.

We were woken by a noise – *Sssssss*!

An enormous snake had made itself into a ring round us and caught us!

After a time, it took one of my friends into its mouth. It didn't bite him, but we saw him going down inside it. For a time we heard his cries. Then they stopped, and we knew that he was dead.

The great snake stayed there all night, and we were afraid to move or to speak. But at last it went away, and we said, "What can we do? It will come back tonight, and it will eat another of us."

We ate fruit and drank water, and we looked for a cave. But there was no good place, and before night we went up a tree to sleep there. I was the stronger man, and I could go nearer to the top of the tree than my friend.

As soon as night fell, the great snake came back, looking for us. It found our tree and came up it. My friend was taken – I heard his last cries from inside the snake – and I was alone.

In the morning, the snake had gone.

"What must I do?" I asked myself. "It will come back tonight and take me. Shall I throw myself into the sea?"

I ate some fruit from the trees, and I thought ... and I thought...

I walked along by the sea. Fortunately there were none of the monkey-men on that island. But I saw very many bits of wood and rope from the ships that they had taken.

I took some very long bits of wood and I put them across my feet, over my head, across my body and along my sides, with bits of rope to stop them from moving. Then I lay down on the ground and waited.

Night came, and I heard the snake.

The great mouth came to my head ... to my side ... to my feet ... to the other side. The wood stopped it everywhere. The snake tried again and again, but it couldn't get me into its great mouth.

At last it moved away, and I gave thanks to Allah. I had been saved again.

In the morning I made a boat out of parts of

ships and bits of wood and rope. I put fruit and water on it, and then I took it out to sea, away from that unhappy island.

I don't want to remember the days on that open boat. I was burnt by the sun and I was thrown about by the sea. But at last I saw a ship far away, and fortunately the sailors saw me. They came and took me up, and they were very kind to me.

The captain and some merchants who were on the ship heard my story.

"We will take you to Basra," the captain said, "but we must go to some other places first. The merchants must sell their goods and buy others, and we must have a good wind to take us back to Basra."

At the next stop, the merchants' goods were brought up.

"Bring up Sindbad's goods," the captain said to his men. "We'll sell them here and take the money to his unfortunate people in Baghdad."

"Sindbad's goods?" I asked. "Do they have this mark on them?" And I made the mark that was always on my goods and boxes.

"Yes," he said. "But how did you know that? The goods have been under all the other goods in the ship for a very long time. The man who owned them died on Roc Island a long time ago."

"He didn't die," I said. And I told him what happened on my second voyage.

It was hard for the captain to believe me, but at last he did believe my story. I sold my goods and bought other goods to sell in Baghdad. So after my third voyage I was a very rich man, and I wanted to live happily in Baghdad.

"There will never be a fourth voyage for me," I thought.

But there *was* a fourth voyage, and tomorrow, if it is the will of Allah, I'll tell you about it.

The Fourth Voyage

One day some merchants came to my house. They spoke about old times, and the voyages that we had made, and the places that we had seen. We remembered the good times and not the bad times.

Soon we were saying that a voyage to the east would be good for us.

I made ready some goods, and we sailed south and east towards the rich lands that we knew. And so we voyaged from island to island and from sea to sea, selling and buying, and seeing one country after another.

We were far from our homeland when one night a great wind threw our ship on its side, and great seas hit it and threw us into the water.

"This is my last hour," I thought, as the ship went down.

But some wood from the ship came towards me, and I put my arms round it. I helped some other merchants and sailors to get on to parts of the wooden ship too.

All next day, the wind and the sea drove us on, but at last we were thrown on land, just alive, but that was all.

We stayed in the same place – just out of the sea – that night because we couldn't move. And we were there when the sun came up and some men found us. I call them men, but they were more like beasts, ugly in face and body.

They took us – hitting and kicking us – to their king. He spoke to them, and they made us sit down. Then they brought food for us. We had never seen food like it, but the other merchants and the sailors ate some. I couldn't eat it. It made me ill to look at it.

How fortunate I was ! That food changed the others. They began to eat foolishly, very quickly and with two hands.

Then I remembered that I had heard about these beast-men. When they catch people from another country, they give them this food. It makes them want to do nothing but eat, so they eat and eat, and become enormously fat. That is how the king and his beast-men like to eat them.

"Stop!" I cried to the men from our ship. But I couldn't help them. They could think of nothing but the food.

Day after day my friends grew fatter and fatter. The beast-men stayed near them and made them eat. Those beast-men saw me becoming more and more ill because I didn't eat anything. But they did nothing to me because they had so many fat people to eat.

"I can't save my friends," I thought, "but I

must save myself. If I stay here and eat nothing, I'll soon be dead."

My friends could never go far from the beast-men – and they never wanted to go far because the beast-men gave them food. But nobody looked at the man who was not fat. So one day I hid under a tree and then moved away into the forest.

After a time I found some fruit that I knew, and I was not afraid to eat it. That food made me a little stronger, and I walked more quickly.

For seven days I walked, and ate fruit, and walked.

At last I saw some men like myself. They were afraid of me, and they came towards me with swords in their hands. But I called to them: "In the name of Allah, hear me!"

I told them who I was and where I came from. And they told me that they came once a year from their own country to that island, but they were always afraid of the beast-men.

"No other man has ever got away from them," they said.

When they went back to their own island, my new friends took me with them. Their king heard about me and wanted to speak to me. He was very kind and gave me a room in his own great house. He sent for me every day and asked me questions about my voyages and about the great city of Baghdad.

His own city was rich in many ways. But I saw one thing that was not so good.

The king and all his people rode horses. They were very good horses, and the people rode well. But they had no saddles.

One day I asked the king, "Why, great king, do you not have a saddle when you ride your horse?"

"A saddle?" he said. "What is that?"

"May I make a saddle for you?" I asked. "Then you will know the answer to your question, and you will see that a saddle is a great help to a man on a horse."

I made a very good saddle for the king and I put it on his horse. He tried it and was very pleased. After that, all the great men of that country wanted saddles, and I made saddles for them. In that way I became very rich, and I was happy to be the friend of the king and of all the great men of the country.

One day the king spoke to me.

"You have become one of us," he said, "and we love you like a brother. There is just one way in which you can come nearer to us."

"Tell me, Oh King," I said. "I am your servant. Your word is the law for me if it is the will of Allah."

"You must be married. There is a woman of great beauty who is very rich, the daughter of one of my friends. You shall marry her."

So I was married at once. My wife was, as the king said, a woman of riches and beauty. But she was more than that: she was one whom I could love, and she loved me, and we were very happy for many weeks.

One day, the wife of one of my new friends died. I went to his house, as a man does in his friend's sad hour. But he was more than sad: he was really ill.

"It is not the will of Allah," I told him, "that a man should be so unhappy when his wife dies. You must be ready to live without her, and—"

"What?" he cried. "Don't you know our rule? It is the rule of this country that the living must go with the dead – the living wife with the dead man, and the living man with his dead wife. This afternoon they will throw my wife's body into the Cave of the Dead, and they will send me down there to die with her."

"It's a very bad rule!" I said.

But that is what happened. That afternoon, the people took the wife's body outside the city. They moved a great stone from a hole in the side of a hill and threw the body down into the Cave of the Dead. Then they tied ropes round my friend and put him down into the cave after her. They put the great stone back over the hole, and soldiers stayed there to stop people if they tried to go near it.

I spoke to the king about it.

Sindbad and his wife are very happy

"It is the rule of the country," he said. "It is a very old rule, and even *I* can't change it."

And then my own dear wife became very ill and died!

The people came to take her body to the Cave of the Dead.

"You can't take me too," I said. "I am not a man of this country, so the rule isn't the same for me."

"Be brave," they said. "You are one of us." And they put ropes round me and took me to the place where the great stone was.

And so I was put down into the cave, and the great stone was put back over the hole, and I could see nothing.

I cried to Allah to save me.

After a time, I found that there was just a little light in the cave. And I saw that they always put the dead into the cave with all their jewels. So there were jewels everywhere in the cave.

There were ropes, too. When the living were put into the cave, the ropes round them were thrown down.

Then I heard something moving. I thought it was a fox, or a beast like a fox. I tried to catch it, but it bit me and ran away.

"If there are beasts here," I thought, "there is another hole that they come through. I must make one of them lead me to it."

I tried to throw a rope round a beast. And I tried again. And again. A thousand times.

At last my throw caught one of them. The beast took me after it towards one end of the cave, a very long way from the part under the great stone. There I found a small hole. A fox could get through it, but I couldn't. So I worked hard to make it bigger. I worked day after day for a long time, and at last I was out in the clean air under the blue sky.

I saw that I was near the sea, at the foot of a great hill. I knew about the place, but I had never been there. The side of the hill was like a wall, and nobody from the city could get up or down it.

I found water in a little river, and fruit on a tree, and I drank and ate. Then I sat down to think.

"I must wait for a ship to come near," I thought – "a ship that is not going *towards* the city. I can wait a long time, because there is food and water here. Shall I go back into the Cave of the Dead to get some of the jewels? If I go back, will I find the way out again?"

I remembered the ropes.

"If I make one very long rope out of a lot of shorter ropes, it will lead me into and out of the cave," I thought.

So I made my long rope, and I went into the cave many times and brought out thousands of jewels. I put them in bags that I made from the cloth that was round the dead bodies. And then I waited for a ship.

At last a ship came to get water from the river.

I told a part of my story to the captain – not all of it, because I was afraid that the people of the city would hear about it. I wanted to give some of the jewels to the captain, but he said: "We are men of Basra. When we find a man who has been thrown by wind or sea on an island, we take him into our ship and give him food and drink and clothes, and we help him on his way to his own country. We never take money or other things from him, because we help him for the love of Allah."

In time, the ship's voyage came to an end at Basra, and I went from there to Baghdad.

My friends were glad to see me, and I gave money and food and clothes to the poor, and help to those who wanted help.

And I said, "Never again! That was my last voyage!"

It was *not* my last voyage, as you will hear, if Allah wills, tomorrow.

The Fifth Voyage

In time, I remembered the good parts of my voyages, I didn't remember the bad parts.

One day I saw men making a new ship – a beautiful ship. I bought that ship, and so I set out, with other merchants, on my fifth voyage, in my own ship.

We sailed from city to city, and from island to island, and from sea to sea, selling and buying and seeing many new places.

One day we came to a very big island where we could see no people, no trees, no rivers. The other merchants went to the land to walk about. They stopped at an enormous white thing like a great dome.

"Don't touch it!" I shouted. "It's a roc's egg. Come away! Quickly!"

But they didn't hear me, or they didn't believe me. They took big stones and made a hole in the side of the egg. There was a noise like a cry from inside the egg: the young roc was dying.

The cry was answered from far up in the sky, and the day became like night as the two great rocs – the father and the mother – flew over.

"They're going to kill us all," I thought.

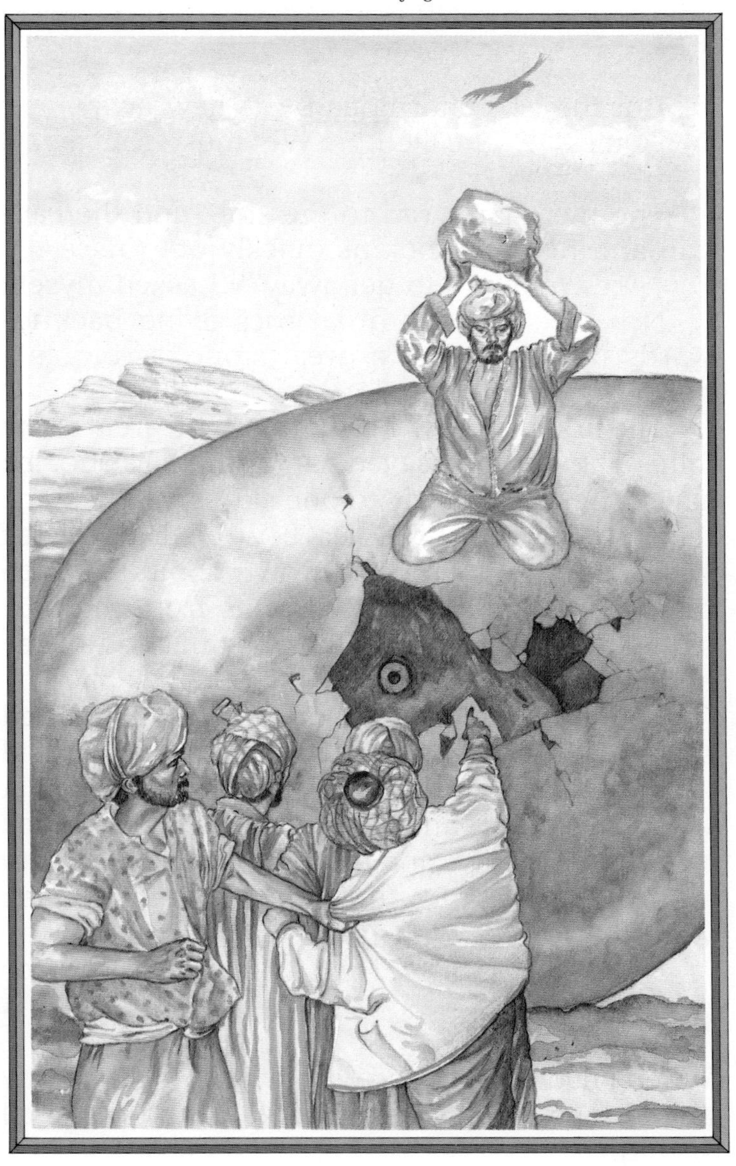

The merchants make a hole in the roc's egg

But the two enormous birds flew away.

"Quickly!" I called. "We must sail away. Run!"

The merchants ran to the ship, and the captain and his men took us quickly out to sea.

"Are we going to get away?" I asked myself.

No. We saw the great rocs flying back towards us. Each had a great stone, as big as a house.

The first bird flew over us, and the great stone fell. The captain saved us from that one: he sailed the ship quickly to one side, and the stone fell into the sea. The sea flew up like hills of water, and the ship was thrown about so much that the captain couldn't save us from the next stone. It fell on us, and that was the end of my beautiful ship.

The stone killed most of the merchants and sailors, but I found myself in the sea, and I found a part of the ship's wooden side near me. That wood saved me, and the wind and the sea took me, after four days and nights, to an island. I saw – and I gave thanks to Allah – a river of clean water, and trees with fruit.

I ate and drank. Then I began to look for people.

When I had gone a little way into the island, I saw an old man. He looked old and ill, and not at all strong.

"Is this an old sailor who was thrown on this

island by the sea?" I asked myself. He was sitting by the side of a small river.

I spoke to him, but he didn't answer.

I spoke again, and he said nothing, but he moved his hand towards the little river.

"He wants me to take him over the river," I thought. And I put him on my back to go across the water.

Then – then he moved very quickly! He put his legs round my neck. His legs were not fat, but they were very hard and very strong. When I tried to make him get off, he kicked me. Then he took my neck in his hands and legs. He was so strong that I nearly died.

It was like that, day after day. At night I could sleep on the ground, but his legs were always round my neck. In the daytime I could only eat fruit and drink water when *he* wanted to. He was always there. He never spoke, but he kicked me to show what he wanted me to do.

One day I found a fruit that makes a very strong drink when it is old. I drank a little and cried out, "Oh, how good! Very good! Ah! I must drink it all!"

The old man kicked me, and I knew that he wanted to try the drink. I gave it to him, and he drank. He liked it, and drank more – and more. His legs fell away from my neck, and I quickly threw him to the ground. Then I took up a big stone and hit his head with it.

After that, I went down to the sea. There was a ship there, and some sailors had come on to the land. I told them about the old man, and they said: "Allah has been good to you! That was the Sheikh al-Bahr, the Old Man of the Sea. No other man ever had the old man's legs round his neck and got away from them alive. He has killed many good sailors in that way. We never come on to this island alone, but always with nine or ten other sailors, because we are afraid of the Old Man of the Sea."

"Why do you come here?" I asked.

"We come for coconuts," they said. "Come with us, and we'll show you. You must have some of these big bags for the coconuts and this small bag, full of stones."

I took the small bag, full of stones, and the big bags, and they led me to a place where there were a lot of coconut trees. These trees grow far up from the ground without any places to put your hands or feet. And the coconuts are all at the top. But there are monkeys at the top.

We threw stones from our small bags at the monkeys. The monkeys were very angry, and they threw coconuts down at us.

Soon we had a lot of coconuts. We cut the outside parts off, and put the nuts into our big bags. When the ship was full of coconuts, we sailed to Comorin and the islands near it. There they paid us well for the coconuts, and we bought wood and other things to take back to Basra.

And so, selling and buying, I came back to my own country richer than when I went away. I gave one tenth of my new riches to the poor, and said to myself: "Never again! There will be no more voyages."

But there *was* another, as you will hear tomorrow, if Allah wills.

The Sixth Voyage

I didn't want to go to sea again. But there were parts of India that I wanted to see, and I took goods and servants and went overland, through the great cities of those lands, selling and buying, and seeing the countries and the people.

At last I came to the end of the road near the mouth of the great river Ganges. There I found a ship which was going on a long voyage to the south and east.

It *was* a long voyage, but not a fortunate one. The wind took us out of our way, and then the sea caught us and took us along with it very quickly.

"Oh!" shouted the captain. "We are all dead men!" And he threw off his turban, and hit his head with his hands. "This is the end!" he cried. "Do you see that great hill? There is a cave at its foot, and it takes the sea into it, with any ships that are on the sea. No man has ever come out of it alive!"

The sailors tried to sail the ship out of the quick-moving water, but – no! – they could do nothing.

Soon we saw the water going into a great cave, quicker and quicker, and it was taking our ship with it. And then – *crash!* – we were in the cave and the ship hit its stone sides. Everything went black.

"I'm dead," I thought, "or I will soon be dead."

But I was not dead. I could see nothing; everything was as black as the blackest night; but I could hear water moving quickly. There was a strong wind. And *I* was moving – moving on something hard, not in the water.

There was no day and no night, but my journey through that black underground place lasted a very long time. In the end I fell asleep and knew nothing.

There was a lot of noise – crying out and shouting. I opened my eyes.

I was on my back, on a small wooden part of the ship. I was at the side of a great river, and a lot of people were looking down at me. The noise came from them.

"Where am I?" I asked.

None of them knew Arabic, but they called a man who did speak a little.

"You are in the land of the great king of Serendip," he told me.

Then I gave thanks to Allah, because I had heard about that great king and his country.

"We come here," the Arabic-speaker said, "to cut waterways to our fields from this river. It comes out of that line of hills. No man has ever

The water takes Sindbad's ship into the cave

been over the hills from here. And no man has ever come from them. How did you come here?"

I told the story of my sixth voyage, and the man who spoke Arabic told it to the others. When I got to the end of the story, they all cried out.

"They say," the man who spoke Arabic told me, "that you must tell this story to the king. We'll take you to him at once."

They gave me food and drink, and then they brought a horse for me. After a journey of three days, we were at the king's city.

In his great hall, the king heard my story. He told his servants to give me rooms near the great hall, and the best clothes, and food and other good things. He sent for me day after day, and I told him the story of my six voyages. He asked very many questions about Baghdad, and I answered as fully as I could.

One day, I heard that a ship had come to the city on its way to Basra. The king said that I could go on it, and he gave me rich presents of gold and diamonds and other jewels.

"Please take a letter and presents from me to the Khalif Harun al-Rashid in Baghdad," he said.

The letter began:

From the King of Serendip, King of the Indies, King of Kings, to his friend, the great Khalif Harun al-Rashid.

And the presents were gold and jewels, and things of great beauty from the forests and fields of Serendip which were never seen in Baghdad.

I had a good voyage to Basra, and I took the letter and the presents to the Khalif. He was very kind to me, and he heard my story and spoke kindly to me.

The Seventh Voyage

I didn't want to make any more journeys or go on any more voyages.

"I'm not young now," I said to my friends. "I'm going to stay at home and be happy in my own house and gardens."

One day I was with my friends when the Khalif Harun al-Rashid sent for me.

"I want you," the great Khalif said, "to take my answer and my presents to the King of Serendip."

"I hear, and I'll go at once," I said.

The Khalif's servants found me the best ship and made it ready for sea. Then, as soon as the wind would take us towards the east, we sailed with the Khalif's letter and the richest presents that anyone can find in Baghdad, Alexandria, Cairo and the cities of the west.

The King of Serendip was happy to see me, and the Khalif's letter and presents pleased him greatly. He was very kind to me, and I began the voyage home with many presents from him and from the great men of his country.

We had sailed for three days when we saw pirates coming towards us. There were hundreds of pirates in five or six boats, and they soon took our ship. They sailed with us to an island, and there they sold us.

I was sold to a merchant, a good man who was kind to me.

"Can you shoot?" he asked me.

"Yes."

"Good. Because the rule in this country is this: when we buy a man from the pirates, he must go to shoot elephants. We sell the tusks and give some of the money to the pirates. I'll take you to the forest tonight, and you can begin."

In the forest, he made me go up a tree.

"Wait there for the elephants to come near, and then shoot one. I will come in the morning and bring you and the elephant's tusks to the city."

I waited a long time, but at last an elephant came near my tree, and I shot it. The merchant came in the morning, and he was pleased to see me and the dead elephant.

"I'm glad you can shoot well," he said. "If you don't kill the elephant when you shoot, he will kill you. Remember that."

That afternoon, I met two men who had been taken by pirates from other ships. Their work, like mine, was to shoot elephants.

"We won't live for long," they told me. "Even if we always kill the elephant, that doesn't save us. The elephants can think, and the friends of the dead elephants soon kill us."

I thought about their words.

"I mustn't go up the same tree twice," I told myself. "I mustn't shoot when more than one elephant is near me. And I *must* kill whenever I shoot."

For a long time, I shot an elephant every night, and I always killed it. The merchant was very pleased.

"You are the best man that I ever owned," he said. "From today you shall have one tusk out of every ten that you get for me. When you have a hundred tusks of your own, you can go home to your country with them."

I had nearly a hundred tusks when, at last, one elephant got away alive after I had shot it.

The next night the forest was full of noise. The elephants – hundreds of them – were looking for me!

Soon there were elephants all round my tree. I went to the top of the tree. The elephants came nearer. I didn't try to shoot, and that saved me. They stood round the tree and just took it out of the ground. They put me on the back of the biggest elephant and walked, one beside another, along valley after valley.

At last we came to a small valley hidden in the hills, and there they stopped. I looked round the valley.

I had heard stories about a place where the elephants all go to die, but I hadn't believed them. I believed them now. Hundreds – thousands of elephants had died here!

The elephants stood round me and looked at me. None of them touched me; they just looked. I began to see that they were telling me something with their eyes.

"If they could speak," I thought, "they would say: 'Why do you shoot us for our tusks? Look here! Look at all these tusks! We don't want them. Take them, and tell the men of the city to stop shooting us.'"

I tried to show the elephants that I knew what they were saying. After that, they helped me to find the way back to the city.

I took the man who owned me to the place where the elephants went to die. He looked, and looked again, and said: "There are as many tusks here as all the merchants in the city can sell in a hundred years!"

They stopped shooting elephants.

They filled a ship for me with tusks to sell in Basra and Baghdad. And I sailed home. That was ten years ago. It was my last voyage. Allah has been good to me!

Sindbad sees the place where elephants go to die

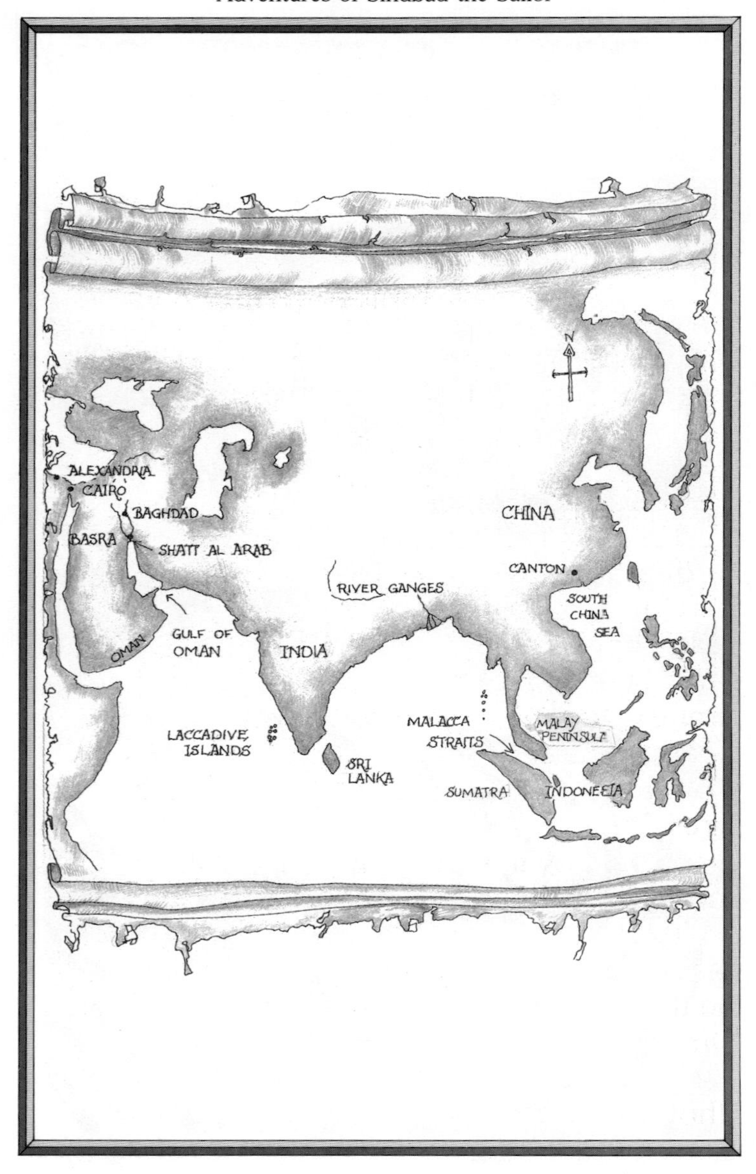
N
ALEXANDRIA
CAIRO
BAGHDAD
BASRA
SHATT AL ARAB
CHINA
CANTON
RIVER GANGES
SOUTH CHINA SEA
GULF OF OMAN
OMAN
INDIA
MALACCA STRAITS
MALAY PENINSULA
LACCADIVE ISLANDS
SRI LANKA
SUMATRA
INDONESIA

A New Sindbad

On 6th July 1981, an Arab ship sailed into Canton in China. Her name was the *Sohar,* and she had sailed to China from Muscat in Oman. Her captain was Tim Severin. The men who sailed her were Arab men of the sea from Oman and scientists from other countries.

Tim Severin is a man who finds the answers to questions by doing things.

One question was: "Could Saint Brendan really have sailed from Ireland to America in an open boat about one thousand years before Columbus?" Tim Severin made a boat just like the boats of Saint Brendan's time, and he sailed it from Ireland to North America. The answer was "Yes."

"Could Arab ships really have sailed to China more than a thousand years ago?"

Tim Severin wanted to know the answer to that question too. "I must make an Arab *dhow,*" he thought, "and I must sail her from the Gulf of Oman to China."

He asked questions and read old books about dhows. There are dhows today, and they *look* the same as the Arab ships of Suleiman al-Tajir's time. But they are not the same. Most dhows today have diesel engines, and the wooden sides and other parts of the ship are fastened with iron.

"We must have a ship that is the same in every way as the ships of Sindbad's time," Severin thought. And he spoke to a lot of people about it.

The Arab ships of a thousand years ago were not fastened with iron. The wooden parts were fastened with strong rope. Very few ships are made in that way today.

"But we must have a ship that is fastened with rope in the old way," Tim Severin said. "It must have no engine. And we must find our way across the seas in the old Arab way."

The great ship-builders of Arabia in the old days were the men of Oman. Sultan Qaboos of Oman and his officers listened to Tim Severin.

"We'll help you," they said. And they helped in every way.

The men of the Laccadive Islands still fasten their boats with coconut rope. Severin brought some of them to Oman to help the Omani ship-builders. He asked old Omani ships' captains how the Omani dhows found their way from place to place across the seas.

By November 1980, the *Sohar* was ready to sail.

She was a good ship, and very strong. Her men found that, with good winds, they could sail three hundred kilometres in twenty-four hours.

But it was hard work.

They met great winds, like the wind in Sindbad's fourth voyage. And there was a time, between Sri Lanka and Sumatra, when there was no wind at all. The ship stayed still, day after day, under the hot sun. Soon they had very little food and water. But the wind came again, and the rain to drink.

They saw no rocs, no enormous snakes, and no pirates (the *Sohar's* men had guns because there *are* still pirates in the South China Sea). But they showed that a ship of Arabia *could* make voyages like those in the Sindbad stories.

Questions

Questions on each story

The First Voyage

1 Where was Sindbad's house?
2 Where did Sindbad's voyage begin?
3 Why did the seamen go on to the island? (To . . .)
4 What was the island?
5 What did Sindbad hold on to in the sea?
6 Where did Sindbad wait for his feet to grow better?
7 Whose horse did he see?
8 How often did the men and horses come to the island?
9 Who was the king of that country?
10 Why did Sindbad tell his story to a ship's captain? (Because . . .)
11 What was Sindbad's present for the king?
12 What did Sindbad do in Baghdad?

The Second Voyage

1 What made Sindbad fall asleep on the island?
2 What was the white thing like a dome?
3 What was the great bird?
4 What did Sindbad use his turban for? (To . . .)
5 Where were the enormous snakes?
6 What was the floor of the valley made of?
7 What do the diamonds stick to?
8 How did Sindbad leave the valley?
9 Why was he rich?

The Third Voyage

1 What did the monkey-men do with the ship?
2 Where did the sailors and merchants go to hide?
3 What did the giant do to the fat man?
4 What did the men do to the giant's eyes?
5 Who threw stones at the boats?

6 How many men reached the island?
7 What happened to two of them?
8 Why didn't the snake eat Sindbad?
9 Where were Sindbad's goods?

The Fourth Voyage

1 What happened to the ship?
2 Why didn't Sindbad eat the beast-men's food?
3 What did Sindbad find to eat?
4 What did Sindbad make for the king?
5 How did he become rich?
6 What happened when a man's wife died?
7 What did Sindbad see in the cave?
8 How did he find the small hole?
9 What did he bring from the cave?
10 Where did the ship take him?

The Fifth Voyage

1 Whose ship did Sindbad sail in?
2 What did the merchants do to the roc's egg?
3 Why did the rocs fly away? (To get . . .)
4 Where was the old man sitting when Sindbad saw him?
5 How did Sindbad escape from the old man?
6 What did the sailors call the old man?
7 How did they make the monkeys throw the coconuts down?

The Sixth Voyage

1 Where did Sindbad's overland journey end?
2 What happened to the ship?
3 What was the name of the country beyond the cave?
4 Where did the people take Sindbad?
5 What letter did Sindbad carry?

The Seventh Voyage

1 Why did Sindbad go on one more voyage?
2 Who sold Sindbad to the merchant?
3 What was Sindbad's work? (He had to . . .)
4 What did the elephants do to Sindbad's tree?
5 What was the small valley?
6 What did Sindbad take to Basra and Baghdad?

Questions on the whole book

These are harder questions. Read the Introduction, and think hard about the questions before you answer them. Some of them ask for your opinion, and there is no fixed answer.

1 Who do you think were the first people to read these stories?

2 Did the first readers believe the stories?

3 Do *you* believe every part of the stories?
a If you don't, say which parts you don't believe.
b What is the difference between you and the first readers?

4 "I was very much afraid on my first voyage."
a Who (in the story) said that?
b Who did he say it to?
c Where were they?
d What happened on the first voyage to make him afraid? (Three things: 1 An island . . . 2 He thought he was alone . . . 3 A man with a sword . . .)
e What was the happy ending to the story of the first voyage?

5 Sindbad escaped from danger in several stories. For each danger in the second column below, answer these questions:
a How did Sindbad escape?
b Was Sindbad clever or fortunate to escape?

Voyage	Danger
2	(a) the great snakes (b) the Valley of Diamonds
3	(a) the monkey-men (b) the giant (c) the great snake
4	(a) the beast-men (b) the Cave of the Dead
5	the Old Man of the Sea
6	the cave
7	the elephants

New words

coconut
a large round fruit from the top of a very tall (palm) tree

diamond
a very hard jewel stone without colour

dome
a round roof on an important building

enormous
very, very big

escape
get away from (a danger)

fortunate
having good things happen to you; lucky

goods
things to sell

merchant
a person who buys and sells things

neck
the part that joins your head to your body

pirate
a seaman who (with others) takes other ships and steals from them

rope
a very strong line, like the line that holds a ship to the shore

saddle
a seat for a rider on a horse

snake
a long creature with no legs, sometimes with a dangerous bite

turban
a long piece of cloth to put round and round a man's head

tusk
one of the two long teeth of an elephant

valley
a length of low land between mountains

voyage
a journey on a ship